Porridge the Tartan Cat

Lochlan

enjoy the Porridge

Adventure

love

Mum & Dad
x

To Jack and Phyllis,
the grooviest grandparents ever! – A.D.

To my three adventurous boys:
Philip, Peter and Paul – Y.S.

Young Kelpies is an imprint of Floris Books
First published in 2017 by Floris Books
Text © 2017 Alan Dapré. Illustrations © 2017 Floris Books
Alan Dapré and Yuliya Somina have asserted their rights
under the Copyright, Designs and Patent Act 1988 to
be identified as the Author and Illustrator of this work

The publisher acknowledges subsidy from
Creative Scotland towards the publication
of this volume

MIX
Paper from
responsible sources
FSC® C117931

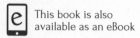

This book is also
available as an eBook

British Library CIP data available
ISBN 978-178250-356-9
Printed & bound by MBM Print SCS Ltd, Glasgow

Porridge the Tartan Cat
and the Bash-Crash-Ding

Written by Alan Dapré

Illustrated by Yuliya Somina

Young Kelpies

1
Greetings from planet Porridge

Hi, I'm Porridge the Tartan Cat.

Once upon a table, I tumbled into a tin of tartan paint! So now I'm the planet's first ever tartan cat. See? I've got more stripes than a tiger on a deckchair.

I live here in Tattiebogle Town with the fantastic McFun family. There's Gadget Grandad, Groovy Gran, Mini Mum, Dino Dad, and the twins: Roaring Ross and Invisible Isla. I'm their owner and look after them all day! At night, I curl up and *cat*-a-log their brawsome adventures. I call them the Big Yins, and they're full of surprising secrets. Why not curl up with me and read all about Groovy Gran?

But please turn the pages quietly.

It's time for my catnap.

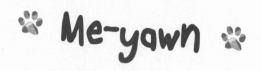

Me-yawn

2

The Chapter After Chapter 1

One morning, just after this chapter had begun, Ross heard a terrifying growl outside the back door.

GRRRRR!

"What was that?" he cried, hiding under the kitchen table.

"That was Porridge growling like a wee dug," giggled Isla.

It wasn't all of me, just my grumpy belly roaring,
FEED ME NOW! I was outside and my food was
inside, so I dashed hungrily towards the cat flap —

THWUMP!

Then I remembered there wasn't one.

❧ Me-owch! ❧

Ross opened the door and peeled me off it with his fingers and a sigh (but mostly with his fingers). He took me inside and soon I was doing my morning exercises – one hundred laps of a milky cat bowl.

❧ Me-licious! ❧

The twins were on the lookout for Gran. She was coming to stay with us because Mum and Dad were going on holiday.

"I can't see her anywhere," said Isla, at the window.

Gadget Grandad would have come too, but this morning he had to go on a secret mission. So secret that I'm not allowed to tell you about it, even in tiny letters.

"Gran always arrives with the same old trolley, wearing the same old clothes," said Ross.

"Gran does *everything* the same old way," groaned his sister. "She's stuck in a groove. She's stuck in a groove. She's..."

"Groovy Gran," giggled Ross.

At the end of their street and this sentence, Groovy Gran appeared, tugging her stubborn trolley. "It's stuck in a groove!"

The twins ran to help. (I would have lent a hand too, but as I don't have any I leant on the gatepost instead and watched.)

They yanked the trolley free, then Groovy Gran gave the twins a bony hug.

As they arrived at the front gate, Groovy Gran's bright eyes swept over my stripes like a barcode scanner. She bent down to give me a cuddle too, her joints cracking like fireworks.

🐾 Me-help! 🐾

Luckily for me, the front door opened and Mum and Dad came out, each carrying a big suitcase.

"See you next week," they cried, stuffing the suitcases into the car boot. "Have fun with Gran!"

They jumped in and set off, waving out of the windows.

Groovy Gran dragged her trolley to the front door, desperate for a cup of tea. "Kids, I'm making you something delicious later."

Ross and Isla looked at each other nervously.

"But... er..." said Isla.

"Aye, plenty of *butter* in your tattie scones."

The twins shuddered. Groovy Gran made tattie scones *every time* she came round. EVERY TIME!

"I need one extra thing," added Groovy Gran. "What's the word now...? You put it on porridge..."

"A collar?" joked Ross, looking at me.

Nope! I knew the answer, because I'm officially the cleverest cat in this story. See?

PORRIDGE IS OFFICIALLY THE CLEVEREST CAT IN THE WHOLE OF THIS STORY – signed _____ Porridge the Tartan Cat

OK, I'm the only cat in this story... but I'm still clever. The answer was: salt. To show the others, I grabbed a shaker with my tartan tail and...

Groovy Gran vanished in a cloud of black pepper.

Me-oops

She sneezed —

BLA-CHOOOOOW!

And her false teeth shot out!

"Where are ma wallies?" she spluttered. (Groovy
Gran calls false teeth 'wallies'.)

I couldn't see them, but...

...I could feel them biting ma bahookie!

3

The Number After 2

Groovy Gran put the kettle on and settled into a chair.

"It's great to have a wee break because of the big hole in the school roof," said Ross.

"I wonder who did it?" said Groovy Gran.

"Maybe a clumsy cat burglar," joked Isla.

Close. It was a clumsy cat. Just *my* rotten luck to fall through the rotten school roof, land on a trampoline and twang back out.

"Och, when I was a lass that roof had more

holes in it than this tea bag," said Groovy Gran. She tossed the soggy tea bag at the bin, but it missed and plopped in her trolley. She reached in, rummaged around at the bottom, and pulled out half a black-and-white photograph. It had clearly been torn in two, many years ago.

Groovy Gran gasped and gawped, her eyes wider than a surprised potato. "I haven't seen this for thirty years! That's me on the left, singing into a microphone. I was in a band, you know."

Isla tried to read the scribbled writing on the back of the torn photo, but it was covered with brown tea stains. "THE BATTY BONES?"

"THE TATTIE SCONES!" corrected Groovy Gran, laughing. "That was the name of our band."

"Were you famous?" asked Ross.

"Aye." Groovy Gran's eyes misted up. Then her glasses misted up too, so she switched off the kettle. "We had ten Number 1 albums, our own tour bus and a mixing desk where I mixed all my ingredients. During each show I'd bake a huge tattie scone tae share with our fans."

Ross studied the photo some more. "Who's that on the drums?"

"That's Biff McBash. He was so good he could drum and knit at the same time!" chuckled Groovy Gran.

"And who's that?" asked Isla, pointing at a girl with wild hair.

"Scruff McDuff, the fastest guitarist in the West... Highlands. Scruff played songs so fast they were over before they even began."

"Cool!" said Isla.

"Is that everyone in the band?" asked Ross.

"Och no. The other half of the photograph is missing so you cannae see Rab McDrab on the triangle. He chose the triangle because he didnae like loud noises."

"Were you loud?" asked Ross.

"Aye, I could sing so loud I raised the roof," chuckled Groovy Gran.

Isla had an idea. "Maybe you could raise money to fix our school roof?"

"You could get the band back together for one night!" blurted Ross.

"We always used to raise money for good causes," said Groovy Gran, dreamily. "But there's a wee problem. Thirty years ago, Rab McDrab left the band in a terrible huff and horrible slippers – we've nae seen each other since!"

At that very moment, a white flash of lightning lit up the kitchen.

I sprang back like a startled cat (because I was startled and a cat). Thunder rolled in the sky – and I rolled into the sink! Isla dried my fur with a towel, and... **whumf!**

I became a fluffy furry round ball.

A pesky robin twittered with laughter on the

window ledge.

"I do miss ma old band mates," sniffed Groovy

Gran, slipping the torn photograph into her pocket.

"It's been so long... I've no idea how tae get in touch with any of them now."

"We'll help you find them, and get the Tattie Scones back on stage for one big gig to raise funds for the school roof," said Ross. "We'll put up posters all over Tattiebogle Town, and get you in the newspaper and on the telly."

"And then we can let the whole town know about it by sending a big hot-air balloon up into the sky!" said Isla airily.

"If only we could play this Saturday. It'll be thirty years tae the day since our last gig," muttered Groovy Gran.

"Great idea," said Isla. "Where would you play?"

"Our usual venue," answered Groovy Gran. "The Crystal Cave, at the foot of Ben Tankle."

"There's no time to waste!" said Ross.

The old lady beamed and her white hair glowed like a sunlit cloud. "When do we start?"

"As soon as we get that poor robin out of Porridge's food bowl," said Isla.

Oops, I wonder how that got in there?

4

Poster Posters

Later that day, I sat on the computer keyboard.

(It's a cat thing.)

"Thanks, Porridge," said Isla, as ma bahookie pressed PRINT. A colourful poster slid out of the printer.

Calling all fans of
The Tattie Scones

Help us find former members Biff, Scruff and Rab so we can put on a **Big Gig** this Saturday!

All profits go towards restoring the Tattiebogle Primary School roof.

Hundreds of posters later, the twins scooped up a pile each and dashed outside, taping them to everything that didn't move: a lamp post, a fence, a lamp post, a bus stop, a lamp post, a stopped bus.

They even taped one to Mavis Muckle and Basil the Elephant, who were waiting at a zebra crossing, wondering if it was for elephants too.

Soon posters were all over Tattiebogle Town, except in puddles because that would be silly. When it began to rain, the twins splashed home, and then wished they hadn't taken a shortcut through a swimming pool.

Up ahead, Anita the Postie found a poster plastered on her bike. She read it and trilled, "Och, I love the Tattie Scones! 'Whoops, There Goes Ma Sporran' was the first song I ever bought – I know all the words!"

Before you could say 'terrific tattie scones', she was singing in the rain and dancing round a lamp post.

Whoops, there goes ma sporran.
Ma sporran did a jig.
It landed on the postie's heid...
Now it's a braw new wig!

The twins giggled. Groovy Gran came out and hummed along. A passing elephant *trump trump trumped* along too, which sounds rude but isn't really.

"I hope Biff, Scruff and Rab see the posters and get in touch," said Isla.

"Aye," said Groovy Gran, and she crossed her fingers for good luck.

I don't have fingers so I pretended I was a black cat and crossed the road instead.

5

Good News!

The rain poured all afternoon because it was rather good at it and liked showing off. So instead of putting up more posters, Isla rang a newspaper reporter and told him about the hunt for Biff, Scruff and Rab. He promised to put the story on the front page of the *Tattiebogle Bugle*. He loved a good scoop.

I love a good scoop too. A good scoop of fishy biscuits in my bowl!

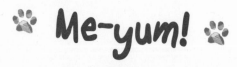 **Me-yum!**

Next, Ross rang the local television studio. Afterwards, he had good news for Groovy Gran.

"Heather McBlether, the presenter of *Tattiebogle Tittletattle*, wants to interview you! We're going to be on the telly tomorrow night!"

"Porridge was on the telly last night," joked Isla.

(Aye, I was, until I fell off.)

Groovy Gran whooped for joy and did a wee jig with a jug. "I'll make us something special for tea while you two go off and play!"

The twins splashed outside and played soccer with a plastic ball. I don't know why. A woolly one is far more fun.

I helped Groovy Gran in the kitchen by whisking up some eggs and flour with my tail. Next time I'll use my whiskers!

Just after five o'clock, the twins came inside, covered in mud.

"It's raining again," grumbled Isla.

"Raining mud?" chuckled Groovy Gran.

"And I lost my football up a tree," grumbled Ross.

"Well, this will cheer you up." Groovy Gran made a plate appear as if by magic (rubbish magic where you just hide something behind your back). On the plate sat two fat tattie scones. "Surprise!"

"Not really," giggled Isla.

"I did try tae cook you both some eggs, but I accidentally made tattie scones instead," sighed Groovy Gran. "Och, this wee one's for you, Porridge."

She dropped a tasty tattie scone with extra fish into my dish. It was gone quicker than you can say tatti—

Just before midnight the rain got bored and went to bed. Groovy Gran let me out into the cold night, but I was still warm because I had my furry coat on.

I was padding along when I heard a loud

That's when I saw a large shadowy creature at the far end of the street.

It was tearing down our posters!

As it came closer, I spotted razor-sharp teeth and claws, and a blunt wet nose.

 Me-woah!

It was a scary hairy Dog of Doom! Or as we say in Tattiebogle Town, Dug o Doom! And – gulp – it was looking at me!

Just after this comma, a tremendous chase began. I sprinted over prickly hedges and prickly hedgehogs and not very prickly puddles. All the while, two shiny yellow eyes followed me like evil car headlights. I zigzagged down the road then scrabbled up a tall oak tree.

Somewhere near the top, I bumped into Ross's lost ball and it fell past me, down on the Dug o Doom waiting below.

I turned and hissed at the hairy menace, and it hissed back!

No, wait – the ball was hissing, firmly stuck in the gnashing hound's gnashers!

The dug chewed feverishly on its football-flavoured gum, then snarled and ran into the darkness –

THWUMP!

– and a tree.

Dugs are so dozy.

I waited until the end of this chapter then dropped on the grass, all alone. (Except for you. Thanks for reading this book by the way.)

Keen to get home, I ran towards the cat flap —

(STILL no cat flap.)

6

The Dug o Doom Strikes Again

Cats don't do mornings. Especially after a night sleeping in the shed.

I had a very long cat stretch, then twanged out of the window. I needed to warn the Big Yins about the horrid hound who tore down the posters last night.

Sadly people aren't smart enough to speak Cat, even though I understand Human perfectly, so I found a torn poster in the street and scampered home to show them the evidence.

The postie was standing at the front door.

KNOCK KNOCK

"Who's there?" said Groovy Gran, on the other side of the door.

"Anita."

"Anita who?"

"Anita tell you something," laughed the postie. "The lamp posts are bare! Your posters are gone!"

Gran swung open the door, I showed her the ripped poster in my mouth and her face clouded over like, um, a cloud.

"Och, Porridge, you wee rascal," she tutted. "Fancy tearing down our posters!"

It wasn't me, I mewed, but nobody understood me.

The twins arrived at the door and tutted too. Even the postie tutted – *and* the pesky robin from Chapter 3. I was well and truly in the dughouse.

That's a really bad place for a cat to be.

"At least people will still read about the band because of Groovy Gran's story in the *Tattiebogle Bugle*," said Isla, full of hope.

"Let's go and buy a copy," said Ross, full of tattie scones. Groovy Gran had made breakfast again.

I sneakily followed them to our local shop and waited outside. As I sunned myself on the kerb, a delivery lorry trundled up, dropped off a stack of newspapers and rumbled away. I was just about to pad over and settle on the papery pile (it's a cat thing) when a grubby grey van swerved straight at me and screeched to a halt. I screeched straight back and leapt for my life! *Och, I've only got nine!*

Two huge paws reached out of the van and snatched the papery pile!

The sight gave me catbumps, which is like goosebumps but with more whiskers and fewer feathers. The dastardly Dug o Doom had struck again!

As the van sped away, one loose copy of the *Tattiebogle Bugle* fluttered about like a rare butterfly. I made a frantic grab for it, but my scrabbling claws chopped it to bits by accident. Wee scraps of white newspaper fell from the sky, like snow with writing on.

"Och, Porridge, you scamp!" Groovy Gran tutted, stepping outside. "We wanted tae read that. There are no papers in the shop!"

"Now no one can read about the Big Gig," groaned Ross.

It wasn't me, I yowled back. *It was that dastardly Dug o Doom.* But they didn't understand. I began to bark like a dog, but nobody got a single woof I said.

I'm rubbish at impressions.

7

Up, Up and Away

My whiskers quivered and tingled all day. I was sure the Dug o Doom would strike again during Groovy Gran's TV interview that afternoon.

The Big Yins still thought it was me who tore the posters down and ripped the papers up, so there was no way they were going to let me tag along. That's why, when a really long car with a really long name arrived to pick them up, I jumped inside and pretended to be a fluffy tartan cushion.

Soon the limousine stopped outside the TV studio. A gruff doorman let everyone in. I ever-so-nearly, almost-not-quite got in too.

"No cats!" the studio doorman snorted when I tried to tiptoe through his legs.

In the blink of an eye I became a furry cushion again. The puzzled doorman picked up the cushion and went inside.

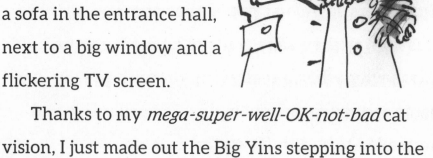

He left the cushion on a sofa in the entrance hall, next to a big window and a flickering TV screen.

Thanks to my *mega-super-well-OK-not-bad* cat vision, I just made out the Big Yins stepping into the lift at the end of the corridor and pressing a button that said:

Floor 4: Studio

"Welcome to *Tattiebogle Tittletattle*," purred Heather McBlether on the screen above me. The camera turned to a packed TV audience full of excited old ladies, who clapped gloved hands and stomped fluffy slippers and hardly made any noise at all.

I sat upright, eager to see Groovy Gran on TV. Instead I saw something scarily hairy appear from the bushes outside!

It was the dreaded Dug o Doom!

The creature threw a rubber bone up at the TV studio roof. My *mega-super-well-OK-not-bad* ears heard it bounce around as if it was in a big round dish. It sounded like a fishy biscuit in my food bowl.

Suddenly the picture on the TV above me flickered and fuzzed as the station signal broke up. Groovy Gran's interview wasn't on – *nothing* was on – the screen was blank. The dastardly Dug o Doom had done a devious deed indeed!

Try saying that one fast...

The dastardly Dug o Doom had done a devious deed indeed!

The dastardly Dug o Doom had done a devious deed indeed!

The television hissed like a tartan cat!

SSSSSSSSSSSS

Hearing the din, the doorman ran in and my luck ran out.

"No animals allowed!" he roared, unaware of the Dug o Doom slinking in behind him, and sneakily taking the lift to the 13th floor.

I had to get past the doorman, fast!

"You're nae cushion," he grunted, prodding my belly. "Where's your zip?"

Here, I yowled, zipping after the dastardly dug. I turned a corner and darted up the stairs.

The doorman soon gave up the chase – too puffed

to go on. I ran up and up until I ran out of stairs and tumbled through a door marked:

Floor 13:
Roof
NO ENTRY

I stumbled across a flat roof and toppled into a huge shiny dish.

Was it full of fishy biscuits? Nope, just Porridge. And a big rubber bone. The dastardly dug had thrown it up here to stop the station's satellite dish from transmitting Groovy Gran's interview!

Keen to fix the situation, I grabbed the bone and tried to climb out of the dish, but the pesky pooch spun the big bowl like crazy!

All the TVs in town went crazy too.

Stop in the name of the paw! I yowled, bouncing around like a coughed-up hairball.

The Dug o Doom howled with laughter and its mighty paws twirled me at the speed of fright.

There was a terrifying

and the dish spun into the sky like a flying saucer!

8

Unidentified Feline Object

What an incredible ride I had! I twirled and swirled to the top of the sky and hovered silently at the edge of space, surrounded by stars and an astronaut called Colin.

Then, all too quickly, I waved goodbye and dropped through the clouds on a helter-skelter belter of a journey down to Earth.

Down,

down,

left a bit,

down,

right a lot,

down,

down

...down towards a wee ant called Basil, who was actually a big *eleph*-ant!

"Look oot, Basil!" said Mavis Muckle, our wheely nice next-door neighbour. They dived inside through their elephant flap just in time!

Three seconds later the dish (and dizzy me) crash-landed in a heap. In Mavis Muckle's stinky, horrible, disgusting, nasty, so-horrible-I'll-say-it-again, horrible revolting compost heap!

I stumbled out, wearing a banana-peel wig and spaghetti whiskers.

"It's an alien from the planet Tartan!" spluttered Mavis, keeking at me from her kitchen window. "W-w-what do you want?"

I stood there with my tummy rumbling and meowed the first thing that came into my head:

TAKE ME TO YOUR LARDER!

By the time Groovy Gran and the twins arrived back home, I had scoffed enough food to feed an elephant.

Mavis rushed outside when she heard the limousine pulling up in our driveway. She was desperate to tell the twins about her alien adventure, and show them the unearthly mess.

"I tried to watch you on the telly," she twittered, "but the picture went funny and then there was a tremendous crash. I ran oot and saw this space alien sitting in a flying saucer!"

She pointed to a very fat cat, sat on the mat by the elephant flap.

"That's just Porridge," said Isla, who knew a down-to-earth cat when she saw one.

"And that's just an uplink dish for transmitting TV shows," said Ross, pointing at the UFO (Unfortunately

Flattened Object). He raised an eyebrow at me. "Our interview never aired because *someone* spun the dish off the TV station roof."

It was that pesky Dug o Doom, I yowled. *Not me!*

"I'm glad no aliens are invading after all," said Mavis, calming down. "This dish will make a braw elephant bath."

"I'm sure Porridge is sorry about the mess," said Groovy Gran. "He's been behaving very oddly recently."

I put on a 'sorry' face, even though the Dug o Doom was to blame!

"What *have* you been up to?" asked Isla, tickling my stripy chin.

The edge of space, I meowed.

"If only cats could talk!" said Ross.

"Let's go home," sighed Groovy Gran. "I'm not sure we'll ever get the band back together now." She gently peeled the banana off my sleepy head, carried me through to the kitchen and popped me in my cosy basket.

It was time for my beauty sleep.

(I don't need long.)

9

All Over The Shop

The next morning, the twins woke me up by clattering into the kitchen like a pair of noisy elephants (but without the trunks or tusks, so not really like noisy elephants at all). They were still keen to find Groovy Gran's bandmates.

"Only a few days to go until Saturday's Big Gig," said Isla, "and we haven't found *any* other band members yet."

Ross sighed. "Or managed to tell the fans about it."

"I hope the Big Gig will go ahead. I love singing," Groovy Gran burbled over the breakfast table.

I love fishy biscuits, I burbled under it.

"I love football," said Ross. "One day, I'll open a shop full of fabuliffic football stuff."

"That reminds me," said Groovy Gran. "Biff McBash once had a woolly idea – to open a drum shop."

Isla jumped up and said (in a chewy voice filled with excitement and tattie scones), "Why don't we see if he has a drum shop now? That's how we can find him!"

"Aye! Why not?" Groovy Gran's eyes twinkled and so did her toes, but no one noticed because she had slippers on.

After breakfast, we looked online for a drum shop nearby but found nothing, so we ran about Tattiebogle Town, looking high and low (I did the low bits).

We searched all day until the cows came home, then searched a bit longer until Basil the Elephant came home too, from his trumpet lesson.

"Och, I cannae see a drum shop anywhere," sighed Groovy Gran.

It was getting dark and the Big Yins were tired, but Groovy Gran wasn't one to throw in the towel or flannel or anything else she'd found in the bathroom.

"Poor Porridge has been searching so hard he's fallen asleep," said Isla, reaching into Groovy Gran's trolley to tickle my ears.

Not sleeping. Listening. Thanks to my *mega-super-well-OK-not-bad* cat hearing, my ears spun and locked onto a faint **BIFF-BASH-CRASH**.

I leapt from the trolley and flew toward the sound like a tartan dart.

"Follow that cat!" yelled Ross, as I disappeared around a distant corner.

Off I ran, through bare streets and hairy legs. The **BIFF-BASH-CRASH** grew ever-louder as I grew ever-closer.

I reached the door of a shop called

The CROCHET and CROTCHET

– a wool shop made from bricks, not wool, which was a shame because I couldn't chase it around.

"Porridge wants us tae go in," said Groovy Gran. With the heart of a lion and the legs of an old lady, she bravely led us in.

"I hope this isn't a wild goose chase," said Isla.

Mmmm. Goose.

Inside, you couldn't move for wool. It was all over the shop. Huge round balls covered the floor and walls. There were strange sticky things sticking out too.

"Are those knitting needles?" asked Ross.

"No, they're Golden Drumsticks!" said Groovy Gran. "They're drumming awards – Biff won stacks of sticks over the years!"

"Then this must be his shop!" shouted Isla.

The biggest and shiniest Golden Drumstick was sticking out of a wall of wool. Behind that wall we heard a **BIFF-BASH-CRASH.**

I gave the drumstick a tug with my tail... and the wall of wool came tumbling down.

Behind it was a wall of noise!

BIFF-BASH-CRASH

BIFF-BASH-CRASH

BIFF-BASH-

CRASHHHHH

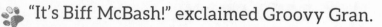

And a squat, bald man with huge arms, biffing and bashing and crashing away on a drum kit – while niftily knitting a scarf!

"It's Biff McBash!" exclaimed Groovy Gran.

I was just about to say that.

10

Drumming Up Support

The moment Biff saw Groovy Gran, sunlight filled the room and birds began to sing.

Mmmm. Birds.

Biff fell off his stool in a lot of amazement and a bit of clumsiness.

"What are you doing here?" he asked.

"Looking for you! What are *you* doing here?" asked Groovy Gran.

"Getting up," said Biff, getting up. "When the Tattie Scones stopped performing, I opened this wool shop. Here I can knit as much as I like, and drum as loud as I like. The wool dampens the sound so no one can hear me."

"Porridge heard you," said Isla.

I purred with pride.

"Clever cat," said Biff, stroking my head. Then he turned to Gran and sighed. "I miss those braw old days with the band."

"Me too," said Groovy Gran.

"We've persuaded our Groovy Gran to get the band together for one last gig," said Ross.

"Will you join me?" the old lady asked Biff.

I gave Biff my *mega-super-well-OK-not-bad* cute floppy-ears and soppy-eyes look.

"Aye, I will!" Biff bashed his drums so hard the whole room rattled and piles of woolly balls cascaded our way.

"We just have to find Scruff and Rab now!" said Groovy Gran.

"And an emergency exit" cried Biff, as giant balls of wool bounced all over the shop.

He yanked another wall-mounted drumstick that opened a hidden door. The others all stumbled out while balls tumbled about.

"Wait – where's Porridge?" shouted Ross.

"Here he comes," whooped Groovy Gran.
I wobbled outside on a huge ball of orange wool.

Mmmm. Wool.

Wool makes me do crazy things! *Sometimes too crazy!*

I careered down the street – leaving a trail of wool behind me that got longer and longer as my ball got smaller and smaller.

Groovy Gran snatched up the loose end and wound it round her fingers.

"Follow that cat!" yelled Ross.

And that, dear reader, is just what they did.

11

Follow That Cat!

The pages flew by as I bounced and bobbled through Chapter 11.

12

Follow That Cat A Bit More!

And wobbled and joggled through Chapter 12.

13

Twirling And Whirling

By the time I got to Chapter 13, the runaway ball of wool had shrunk to the size of this full stop.

I had bounced right out of town and into a tattie field, surrounded by giant rocks. All alone, apart from a tatty *tattiebogle*. Before too long, Biff and the twins joined me, followed by Groovy Gran – who looked *very wound up.*

Aye.

Very wound up in all that orange wool she'd been collecting!

"We'll save you," cried the twins.

They each grabbed a leg and pulled her free. The orange ball trundled off down a slope, never to be seen again – well, not until Chapter 23 anyway.

Biff asked Groovy Gran if she was OK.

"Never felt better," she replied, still gently spinning in circles. "All this twirling has got ma brain whirling. I know exactly what tae do next."

Munch some fishy biscuits? I mewed hopefully.

"We must find Scruff McDuff," the old lady declared.

Biff's face crumpled like a sad paper bag. "It's going to be a terribly long, hard, difficult task," he wailed. "No one has seen Scruff for years. She could be absolutely completely totally anywhere in the whole wide world. Or on Jupiter. Or lost in outer space in a black hole without a torch. We're doomed, I tell you. Doomed!"

"Hello," said a new voice.

"I do believe that's Scruff McDuff!" said Groovy Gran, looking around. "What luck!"

Ahem.

Luck had nothing to do with it. It totally wasn't a coincidence. I had cleverly steered my ball of wool into Scruff McDuff's field and saved the day. *And* saved us having to search for her for ages and pages!

Me-phew!

14
Ka-bla-dang!

We peered through the murky twilight at the scruffy tattiebogle. Sleepy bats were hanging from its guitar.

"Say something," said Biff to the tattiebogle.

"Or play something," said Groovy Gran.

The tattiebogle twanged a note so high and sharp that the bats went batty and wheeled and squealed into the darkness.

"Bless ma cotton socks, it really *is* Scruff McDuff," cried Biff, knitting two cotton socks in delight. "Are you a tattiebogle now?"

"Yes, but I dinnae scare off birds, I scare off bats. I'm the world's first and only *batty*bogle," said Scruff, surrounded by giant rocks that we suddenly realised were loudspeakers! "Out here I can play my guitar REALLY loud! I call this place 'Tattie Sconehenge.' It's great, but not as great as playing with the *real* Tattie Scones."

She rumbustiously strummed an old chart-topping hit, and Groovy Gran burst into song:

Och, I miss ma misty mountain,
And ma misty misty loch,
And ma misty misty misty road,
To ma misty misty misty misty broch!

The twins danced while the big speakers wailed
like stripy tabby cats and threw a ten-minute,
million mega-watt tantrum.

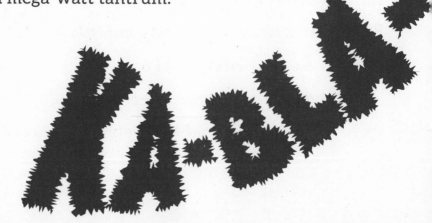

KA-BLK!

DANG!

I wailed like a stripy tabby cat, too. Only more tartany.

"That song nearly blew my eyebrows off," laughed Biff, who didn't mind because he could always knit some more.

When the rollicking racket finally faded, the three old friends hugged and began telling the twins stories from long ago, which they couldn't quite remember properly so they made up some bits.

I was feeling pleased with myself for reuniting them when I spotted something in the shadows that made my heart freeze and my toes go a bit chilly.

Something on the far side of Tattie Sconehenge was nudging a towering speaker.

One sneaky push later, the speaker fell forward and struck a second, which thumped into a third. One by one, the huge blocks toppled. And when the last one crashed down it missed me by a whisker!

I hid behind Isla.

"Poor Porridge," she cooed.

"We must really **rock** to have knocked over that block," laughed Scruff.

If only I could tell them it was the dreaded

Dug o Doom! I wagged my tail and ran in circles like daft dugs do.

"Porridge is acting very strangely today," said Isla.

"This place is very strange too." Ross shivered. "Let's get out of here!"

15
Donk!

We all met for a tattie scone breakfast the next morning, and Groovy Gran told us about the last ever Big Gig the Tattie Scones did before they broke up.

"One dark and stormy Saturday night thirty years ago, I was singing as usual by a giant oven while Biff played drums on top. Scruff was strumming her guitar alongside Rab McDrab, whose one job that night was to tap his triangle when the last song ended."

DING!

"We had it all perfectly planned: the oven door would open and a huge tattie scone would slide out. The fans would go wild and everyone would take a delicious chunk home for supper."

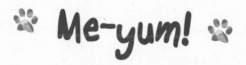

Me-yum!

"Only it didn't happen," sighed Gran.

Scruff took over the story: "There wisnae a DING. Not even a DING. Or a DING."

"Some say Rab forgot to tap his triangle," said Scruff. "Others say he had fallen fast asleep."

Groovy Gran continued. "After the show there was a row and Rab McDrab stormed out, never to be seen again. Not even in panto."

"I wonder what he's doing now?" said Isla.

Biff answered softly, "A long time ago, a friend of a friend of a friend, who wisnae a friend but lived next door tae a friend of a friend, said that Rab took a job in a factory. I don't remember what kind of factory. Ma mind has gone woolly over the years."

I impatiently pawed at my empty food bowl in the hope someone would fill it.

My sharp claw tapped against the rim:

DING!

Biff leapt to his feet! "Now I remember! Rab got a job testing food bowls: perfect bowls go DING, duds go DONK."

Groovy Gran gasped. "I used tae play outside the gates of a food-bowl factory when I was a wee lass."

"Do you remember where it was?" asked Ross.

"It was all so long ago." Groovy Gran sighed wearily, feeling as old as the Hills. (Mr and Mrs Hill lived over the road and were 122 last year.) "All I remember is that it had a wonky chimney."

Everyone sat in silence.

No one moved.

It was like a rubbish game of musical statues without the music.

Groovy Gran simply could not remember, so it

was up to me – Super Porridge! – to find the bowl factory and SAVE THE DAY.

Again.

It would be rude not to. The first step, as always, was to sniff out some fishy biscuits.

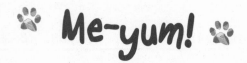 **Me-yum!**

Sniff

Sniff

16
The Factory

Sniff

Sniff

While everyone was staring at a map of Tattiebogle
Town, I sniffed the air with my nose (because it
was better than sniffing with my ears) and smelt
something fishy far away.

I burst through the middle of the map and landed
on a spare suitcase in the hall.

"Porridge is on the case," laughed Ross.

True. Then I was on a flowerpot, then a fence, and
then a long winding path. The Big Yins chased after me

Sniff

Sniff   *Sniff*

as I ran like the wind down Windy Wynd and arrived at Windy Wendy's Pet Shop.

Wendy was a jolly lady and full of beans, which is why she was called Windy Wendy. (Let me tell you a wee secret. She is not as nice as she seems, but that's another story! You'll have to read *Porridge the Tartan Cat and the Kittycat Kidnap* to find out more!)

Isla pointed to a sign in the pet shop window that read:

"Is that why we're here?" groaned Isla. "Porridge, you're supposed to be *helping*, not shopping for fishy biscuits!"

I shook my head. We had to find the factory and I hoped this pet shop would give us a wee clue. When we went inside, we were hit with the stink of a thousand skunks. I held my nose and scouted around for some pet bowls to show her.

At last I found a box containing twenty! I pointed my tartan tail at a label on the top flap.

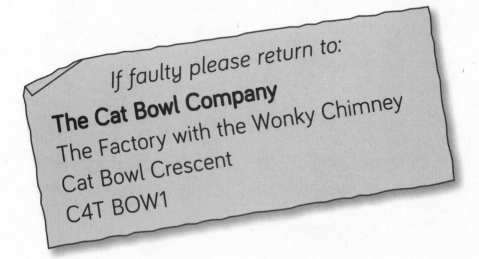

If faulty please return to:
The Cat Bowl Company
The Factory with the Wonky Chimney
Cat Bowl Crescent
C4T BOW1

"Well done, Porridge!" yelled the twins together.

"I'll find 'Cat Bowl Crescent' on the map," said Ross, holding it up for all to see. "This pet shop is very close to Very Close, which is ever so close to Everso Close."

"But where is Cat Bowl Crescent?" asked Biff.

"Somewhere in this Porridge-shaped hole," sighed Ross, poking his head though the bit I twanged through earlier.

Me-whoops!

"If we're going tae find this factory we need a sign," said Scruff.

"There's one," grinned Groovy Gran, pointing out of the pet shop window.

The number 48 trundled...

...very close to Very Close

...and ever so close to Everso Close

...before it turned lazily into Cat Bowl Crescent. The curving road was lined with wrinkly old trees and wrinkly old pensioners at bus stops.

"There's the wonky chimney!" whooped Groovy Gran.

We hopped off the bus by a big factory gate and Groovy Gran jangled a dangly bell.

We waited for ages and ages and... you're probably better off going straight to Chapter 17 than hanging around here.

See you later.

17

Later

A plump, grey-faced lady ambled across the cobbled factory yard. She wore a long grey coat and her hair was pulled into a round bun that would taste horrible if you ate it.

"I'm Dawn McYawn, the manager," she yawned. "Can I help you?"

"I do hope so," trilled Groovy Gran. "We're looking for Rab McDrab."

The factory manager circled Groovy Gran slowly and gave her a long, thoughtful look. When Dawn McYawn spoke next, her words tumbled out like acrobats. "I know you! You were in Rab's band! The Scatty Bones!"

Groovy Gran roared with laughter and bent over until she nearly snapped. "It was the Tattie Scones!"

Dawn McYawn reddened like a ripe tomato and probably wished the ground would swallow her up or at least nibble her toes.

I coughed loudly to remind everyone why we were here. (And to get rid of a furball!)

"We're supposed to be re-forming the band for a Big Gig on Saturday," said Scruff. "Do you know where we can find Rab?"

Dawn told them all she knew. "Aye, Rab worked

here a long time ago when this was a dug-bowl factory. He used to walk about town advertising our dug bowls. Then the factory began making cat bowls instead, and Rab was made Chief Dinger. But something about the cat job chimed badly with him. One day, Rab slipped out of the factory never to return! Or say goodbye! Or shut the gate!"

Groovy Gran spluttered. "Rab always shut gates."

"There's more to the story. Come with me," yawned Dawn. The manager led us into her grey office and opened a wardrobe full of grey coats hanging on hangers. Dawn McYawn picked one out. "This is my favourite."

The twins giggled. It was grey just like all the other grey coats. I spun on my tail with boredom.

What did this have to do with Rab McDrab?

But as soon as Dawn lifted out the grey coat, its triangular hanger started to play a wee tune.

"Ooh, a musical coat hanger," gushed Groovy Gran. "I've always wanted one."

"So have we," said the twins.

"They're sold out everywhere," said Biff.

"I need one!" added Scruff.

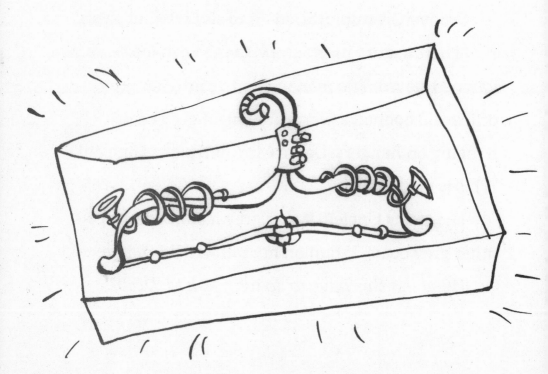

"Rab came up with the idea from his triangle-playing days," explained Dawn. "He thought *all* triangle shapes should make music. And they should be able to do more than DING. Apparently his marvellous invention has made him so rich that he now lives in a whopping big mansion high on a hill, miles away, just over there."

The factory manager waggled her pudgy fingers through the window at a whopping big mansion high on a hill, miles away, just over there.

"It *is* whopping," said Isla.

"And big," said Ross.

"And high on a hill, miles away, just over there," added Groovy Gran, who knew such things because she was old and wise and had eyes. "I think we need tae pay it a visit."

18

The Whopping Big Mansion High on a Hill, Miles Away, Just Over There

It was noon o'clock when we crunched up a gravel driveway in search of Rab McDrab.

"I've found a clue," said Ross, eyeing something big and shiny with four glinting wheels. It looked more like a car to me.

Ross read out the polished registration plate.

MC DR4B

"I know this car. Rab bought it after our first hit song," said Groovy Gran. "He thought the bumper looked really smily."

"It does," said Isla, looking really smily too.

The Big Yins stood by a large oak door. Isla climbed on her brother's shoulders and pressed a gold doorbell. Somewhere inside the whopping big mansion, high on a hill, *not* miles away but just over here, a bell tinkled.

⁺tinkle⁺

No one came.

We waited a long time.

We waited a *very* long time.

A time so long you could down put this book and play with your pal next door and have supper then go to bed and wake up the next day and still be waiting!

Scruff shouted, **"IS ANYONE THERE?"** in big letters through the big letterbox. "Not a sausage," she sighed, turning to walk away.

There's a sausage in Chapter 24, I meowed from inside the mansion.

Inside the mansion?

"Look – another tartan cat!" shouted Scruff, pressing her nose against the wee round window.

"No, it's Porridge!" laughed Isla. "How did you get in there?"

Easy peasy Porridge squeezy, I purred and vanished from view.

The large letterbox flap swung open and I squeezed back outside with a folded *Tattiebogle Bugle* in my mouth.

"That's a funny cat flap," giggled Ross. He opened up the newspaper and read the headline.

COME AND JIG AT THE BIG GIG! THE TATTIE SCONES ARE BACK!

"Where did you find it?" asked Isla. I pointed to the round window and she peered in to see a stack of unread newspapers next to a heap of ripped posters. "*That's* where they went."

Suddenly a hairy beast with fiery eyes peered back at her!

The Dug o Doom!

Groovy Gran and Biff quickly crouched behind Gran's trolley. The twins and Scruff hid behind a tulip.

CRASH!

The thick oak door flew open and splintered against a marble pillar. Out stormed the Dug o Doom, prowling and scowling and growling and bowling.

Aye, bowling!

The horrible hound bowled an ornamental stone ball down the steps towards us. It smashed into the old car outside. The bumper fell off and landed upside-down with a frown.

Now for the scary part of my story.

The Dug o Doom bellowed and the Big Yins ran for their lives!

I ran for my lives too – all nine of them.

19

A place To play

At the end of the drive, the birds were tweeting happily on their phones and it was all very peaceful.

Until we *thundered* down the road like *lightning* and *hailed* a bus and *stormed* on board.

We nearly mist the bus! I joked, using up the last of my weather puns.

"Down boy!" cried Groovy Gran as the Dug o Doom snapped at the half-open bus door. She scattered a bag of Soor Sucker sweets under its paws. Down it went.

 **Me-phew!**

Soon it was just a hairy dot in the distance.

Back at the house, Groovy Gran lit a cosy fire and the abominable nightmare we'd just experienced melted away like a not-very-nice snowman.

"That's it then," sighed Biff. "We couldn't find him. No Rab, no Big Gig."

And no fishy biscuits, sighed me.

I gave my bowl another sad

DING!

"Och, thanks Porridge," said Scruff. "Here's an idea: if we don't find Rab, we just get someone else to DING at the BIG GIG?"

"Porridge can DING his cat bowl!" blurted Groovy Gran. "Then the oven will open and all the fans will go wild. Piece of cake, I mean, tattie scone. What do you think, Porridge?"

Great idea.

I gave my bowl another quick

DING!

and Ross filled it with fishy biscuits, AT LAST!

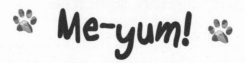

"We still need to tell people where and when the gig will be," said Isla.

"Aye, so let's check out the old venue first," cried Scruff.

Groovy Gran leapt from her chair, crackling with excitement and arthritis. With no time to waste, and just days before the Big Gig, we hurried off. In the rush, a box of fishy biscuits was knocked over. I helpfully stayed behind a wee moment to sort out the mess.

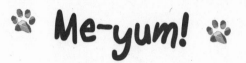 **Me-yum!**

They can thank me later.

20

Dang. Dung. Ding!

Groovy Gran led us along a long winding path to the Tattie Scones' favourite venue: the Crystal Cave at the foot of Ben Tankle. And no one got a bent ankle.

 **Me-phew!**

By now, the evening sun was hovering outside the cave, but the light dared not go in as it was a wee bit dark and blocked by creepy creeping vine creepers.

Ross and Isla pulled them apart like lush green curtains, keen to see inside.

Safe in Ross's rucksack, I peeked nervously into the cave and the darkness stared back, which was a bit rude.

"I'll turn on the light," said Groovy Gran. She grasped a long metal lever and yanked it down towards her whiskery chin.

Somewhere in the gloom, a noisy power generator rumbled into life.

Giant glass bulbs began to glow, spreading a warm light all over the Crystal Cave. It glittered like Santa's grotto and everything was shiny and bright as Rudolph's nose after a polish.

"What is *that*?" cried Ross. He scampered over to a huge metal cube in the centre of the cave.

"*That*, laddie, is the biggest tattie scone oven in the whole galaxiverse," said Biff proudly. "I knitted it from 9,999 balls of wire wool. It's looks a little rusty these days, but should still work."

"How does it work?" asked Isla.

"It's sound-operated," said Groovy Gran. "Only a perfect DING can open it. Sadly Rab isn't here and Porridge doesn't have his food bowl."

I guess you know what's coming next. I had to save the day. I'm cool with that. It's my job.

I searched the ground and found two crystals. When I bashed them together they unfortunately went

DANG!

So I found two dung beetles. Och, you can guess what sound they would make.

DUNG!

I was scratching the back of my ear for an answer when I caught my claw on the metal name tag on my collar. It's under so much tartan fluff I'd forgotten it was there.

DING!

The sound echoed around the Crystal Cave and bounced against the huge oven. To my surprise, its rusty old door swung down like a castle drawbridge and struck the marble stage!

"You opened the oven!" whooped Ross, rushing inside.

Aye, I meant to do that. Sort of.

His heart skipped and his feet joined in when he saw the treasure trapped within. "Look Isla, it's a tattie scone as big as a house!"

"It's incredible!" spluttered Isla.

"It's inedible," said Groovy Gran, rapping it with her knuckles. "It's been here since the night Rab left the band. Nae worries, we'll drag it oot and make a fresh one at the Big Gig."

Thanks to the magic of story-writing, it took just one sentence to shove the huge old tattie scone outside. Biff whipped out his knitting needles and began scraping and chipping and scratching and gouging (and other words ending in *ing*). No one could guess what he was doing-ing.

"Give us a sign," said Ross.

"I will," said Biff.

True to his word, he did. And what a mighty marvellous sign it was too.

"Our fans will see those letters from miles away," cheered a delighted Scruff.

21
A Lot of Hot Air

With so little time until the big gig, the Big Yins were busy as bees and other letters of the alphabet.

Scruff made notes about the notes she had to strum, and Biff knitted himself a new drum kit. The twins created cool dance routines and hired a huge hot-air balloon to advertise the gig! Meanwhile, Groovy Gran practised her old songs until she knew them backwards, but they sounded a bit silly, so she practised them forwards instead.

As for me?

I dozed the whole time, so I would be fresh as a daisy. Not Daisy who stands in a muddy field and goes **Moo**. The other one.

When I awoke on the morning of the Big Gig, the house was quiet as a mouse.

Mmmm. Mouse.

Where was everyone? Surely they wouldn't have gone without me? I crawled out of the chimney and padded along the roof, quiet as that mouse you keep reading about.

Mmmm. Mouse.

No one was about, so I started looking for that pesky mouse. Suddenly there was a loud squeak above my head.

Mmmm. Mouse.

I licked my lips and looked up.

"Hi Porridge!" called Ross. He and the others were bobbing above the roof in a wicker basket. It hung from a hot-air balloon that was pushed along by a squeaky propeller.

The great gasbag circled lower and lower and Biff scooped me up in his chunky arms.

"Welcome aboard," cried Groovy Gran. Then she tossed out a plump sandbag and the tartan balloon soared away from the house, trailing down some guy ropes (named after some guy).

I was worried that the Dug o Doom would try to stop us from telling people about the gig like he had every other time, but there was no sign of him.

🐾 Me-phew! 🐾

Every once in a while, Groovy Gran pulled a wee lever and heated the gasbag with a jet of flame. Each jet sent the balloon higher over Tattiebogle Town.

"I see ma old field," said Scruff. On the ground below us, we could make out a circle of speakers, tumbled over like dominoes. Biff cranked a handle and the squeaky propeller picked up speed.

A crowd had begun to gather in the High Street. They marvelled at the sight of something plump, round and tartan filling the sky.

Not *me, the balloon!*

Just then, Isla released our giant message so the whole town could see:

THE TATTIE SCONES PLAY TONIGHT AT THE CRYSTAL CAVE! EVERYONE WELCOME, INCLUDING ELEPHANTS!

22

Mission Impussible

The big gasbag advertised the Big Gig all day long! We watched from above as eager fans flocked to the Crystal Cave. Evening came and the clumsy sun slipped on a waxed moon and it all went dark.

"If only Rab McDrab was here to perform with us tonight." Groovy Gran sighed. She turned down the flame and let the balloon sink slowly towards the venue, while she serenaded us with a delicious song about salmon.

Mmmm. Salmon.

Scruff strummed along and my tummy rumbled along.

Then, without warning, a heavy metal claw hooked the side of the basket and we were all tossed about like a salad!

A long rope dangled from the claw.
My sharp eyes followed it downwards
and spied –

🐾 **Me-gulp!** 🐾

– the dreaded Dug o Doom!
The pesky pooch was looping
the far end of the rope around
the pointed peak of Ben
Tankle! The balloon was going
nowhere stuck to a mountain!

But I was going somewhere.

I was going on a mission, to slide
down the rope and yank the loop free and
release the balloon!

🐾 **Me-WHOOSH!** 🐾

As I neared the ground, I yanked the loop at the end of the rope. The loop flew off Ben Tankle peak – and accidentally lassoed the Dug o Doom's tail!

Me-oops!

The rising balloon lifted the pooch off its paws. Desperate to hold onto something, it grabbed my collar –

Me-help!

– and pulled me off the rope! I dangled below the Dug o Doom, above a deadly drop!

Me-AAAAAAAARGH!

Lucky for me, the twins knew what to do.

"Quick, rock the basket!" they cried. Everyone ran side to side.

The more they rocked, the more the rope swung! It was all too much for the weary Dug o Doom. On a big swing upwards, it finally let go!

Me-WHOOSH!

"Is it a bird? Is it a plane?" said Scruff, as I flew towards the basket.

"No, it's Porridge, of course," cried Groovy Gran, catching me in her long-handled trolley.

Me-phew!

Isla plucked me out and hugged me until I squeaked like a rubber mouse.

Mmmm. Mouse.

23

Guess Who?

Now the Dug o Doom was safely lassoed below us, there was no time to lose. The Tattie Scones were already late for their Big Gig!

"Time to drop in on our fans," said Groovy Gran. She let out some air from the giant gasbag and we quickly lost height.

A big "OOOOH" went up from the crowd as the balloon spiralled down toward the Crystal Cave.

"We're landing too fast," gasped Groovy Gran.

"That dangling dug is weighing us down."

"Hold on to your hats!" shouted Biff.

And cats! I yowled.

With a howl of rage, the Dug o Doom climbed up the rope like a big hairy spider. He came up over the basket, leapt higher and tore a hole in the balloon, which let out a rude raspberry (the kind that would get you into trouble if you did it at school).

Flurrrrrplurplurplurrrrpppp!

With no air inside, the balloon fell to Earth like a clumsy hippo. The basket hurtled into the cave, bounced off the oven, skated across the smooth marble stage, and scored nine 6's from the crowd for artistic impression (which is really good).

But what of the Dug o Doom?

He had bitten through the rope attached to his tail and made a wild dash for freedom. But as he tried to get away, the big orange ball of wool from Chapter 13 thundered into the cave and rolled right over the horrid hound.

Now the Dug o Doom was all wrapped up like an unwanted present.

The crowd broke into wild applause, convinced that the falling balloon and the dug were all part of the show.

"I want a word with this pesky dug's owner," muttered Groovy Gran, rushing over really really slowly because old people do that. Really.

Dug owners put their phone numbers on dug tags because dugs are always running off. To find the dug tag on the Dug o Doom's collar, I dug through layers of wool. But the collar was sewn onto the dug's moth-eaten fur.

Sewn?

Hmmm. There was a wee tag hanging from the collar, shaped like a dug bowl. It said:

Then I spotted a metal zip running up the dug's tummy. Suddenly it all made sense. This was no dug, but a pesky person inside an old dug costume, used to advertise dug bowls long ago.

Who was inside? It had to be someone who had worked in the factory before it made cat bowls. My cat senses tingled and my bell jingled. I knew it! The person in the costume had to be –

Dawn McYawn!

I tore through the orange wool and scratched off
the hairy costume head to reveal...

"RAB McDRAB!" gasped Groovy Gran.

 Me-oops!

Aye, it was Rab, not Dawn. *My mistake.*

"Ay caramba!" Biff shouted, in surprise and Spanish.

"What have you got to say for yourself?" tutted Isla. "Trying to crash our balloon and scaring people..."

And cats.

Rab sniffed and wiped his wet nose with a furry paw. "Sorry. It was me who tore doon the posters. And snatched the papers. And spun that big dish into space. And tried to anchor you to Ben Tankle. And then burst your balloon."

That was a lot of ands.

"We thought it was Porridge playing tricks." Groovy Gran tutted.

I tutted too.

"But why did you do all that?" asked Ross.

"I didnae want the Tattie Scones tae gig again," sobbed Rab. A tear dangled off his nose like a shiny tree bauble. "Last time, you said I didnae DING my triangle. But I did. It wisnae my fault the triangle made nae sound when I struck it."

If only he could prove he was telling the truth!

Scratch

24
Proof

Scratch

Scratch

Scratch

I scratched my itchy neck and found half a torn photograph lodged in my collar! It must have got stuck there when Groovy Gran caught me in her trolley. I held it out on my claw.

"Look at that! And I've got the other piece in ma pocket." Groovy Gran quickly joined up both halves like a two-piece jigsaw puzzle.

Scratch

My *mega-super-well-OK-not-bad* eyes zoomed

Scratch

Scratch

in on the grainy image of the band, and I spotted something no one had seen before: a missing link that explained why the triangle didnae DING! I quickly clawed a circle around it.

"What's that in Rab's hand?" asked Isla, squinting.

"A link sausage!" gasped Groovy Gran.

"That was ma after-show snack," whispered an embarrassed Scruff. "I dinnae like tattie scones much."

Groovy Gran gave a flabbergasted gasp! Which is hard to say fast.

Groovy Gran gave a flabbergasted gasp!
Groovy Gran gave a flabbergasted gasp!

"I must have grabbed the sausage in the dark," sighed Rab.

Groovy Gran giggled. "You hit the triangle with a sausage?"

 Rab's face brightened. "Aye. I may have made a wee mistake, but this photo is proof I did NOT forget to DING that day."

"Sorry Rab," said Groovy Gran, and she hugged him like he was the best Christmas present ever (like a scratching post or a truck full of fishy biscuits)!

The excited fans began to chant, impatient for the gig to begin.

"I didn't bring a triangle with me!" said Rab, flustered.

I handed over my collar with its metal name tag.

"Porridge wants you to hit the tag," said Isla. "It makes a delightful DING!"

Rab's look of surprise gave way to happiness, but then to despair. "Och, I still need a metal dinger!" he spluttered. "I know I had one around here somewhere, thirty years ago."

Cats don't usually play fetch, but in this case I made an exception. Quick as runny porridge, I dived under the mixing desk and just a few words later, I spotted it.

"You fantabulous feline!" cried Rab, when I dropped the dinger in his paws. He wagged his tail, padded to the front of the stage and held his dinger so high it glittered under the bright lights, like the legendary sword Excalibur. And some people actually got down on one knee. Maybe they were knights? Or doing up their shoelaces.

"It's showtime!" cried Rab, grinning so brightly that the front row put sunglasses on. He nodded at Biff, who bashed his drums.

BIFF-BASH-CRASH

The Big Gig had begun!

25

What A Show!

"This is the best gig EVER!" said Ross, dancing beside Isla.

Biff bashed and crashed his drum kit on top of the oven, Scruff jangled her guitar strings and Rab tapped his hairy feet along to the beat. Meanwhile Groovy Gran strutted behind the mixing desk, stirring ingredients and singing like a bird.

Mmmm. Bird.

Even after thirty years, the fans still knew every

word. Except for Mavis Muckle's friend Doris Prune, who just pretended she did.

Anita the Postie danced by the stage and tossed fan letters to the band. Mavis Muckle sang from the bottom of her heart and Basil trumped from the heart of his bottom. Doris Prune waved her hat in the air (because elephants can be *really* smelly).

After three songs, Groovy Gran dolloped her mega-mix onto a big tray dish. Then eager volunteers surged onto the stage and helped slide it into the oven. They swung the door shut and Groovy Gran turned the temperature up to ELEVEN.

The tattie-scone mix rose and plumped up like an incredible edible balloon. After nine songs, it was bigger than a shed. After twelve songs, it was bigger than a shedload of sheds!

The Crystal Cave really rocked as the fans jumped in time to the music. So did a bag of self-raising flour. It fell onto the floor and a chalky cloud billowed up around the band.

Groovy Gran turned white as a ghost and spluttered and coughed so much her slobbery choppers whirled off into the crowd.

"I've lost ma wallies," the old lady croaked, desperate to get her false teeth back. "I cannae sing without them!"

There was only one thing I could do.

Read a book?

Eat fishy biscuits?

Catch a pesky robin?

OK, so there were lots of things I could have done – but only one thing I *had to* do. I leapt off the stage into a sea of fans, tossed about like a ship with whiskers.

Groovy Gran's voice was now just a thin sloshy

whisper. She needed those wallies back!

"Quick, let's help," said Isla.

The twins grabbed a microphone each and got in on the act.

Whoops, there goes ma haggis,
Ma haggis just went splat.
It landed on the teacher's heid...
Now it's a braw new...

I saw the wallies bounce off Basil's trunk and I batted them back towards the stage with my tartan tail. Groovy Gran opened her mouth in astonishment and the wallies plopped right in. She belted out the last word...

HAT!

On cue, Rab swung his metal dinger and my name tag went **DING!**

26
We Did It!

The oven door opened and an enormous tattie scone slid out. A gorgeous aroma made the audience dribble – even the babies (but no one noticed, as they dribble a lot anyway).

What a glorious golden colour the tattie scone was too. Timed and baked to perfection.

"You did it," cried Groovy Gran, giving Rab a hug.

"*We* did it," he shouted, proudly placing my name tag around my neck as if giving me a medal for being fantabulous, which I am by the way. Rab told me in Chapter 24.

PORRIDGE THE TARTAN CAT WINS GOLD FOR SCOTLAND IN THE FANTABULOUS FELINE COMPETITION

"We've raised enough money to raise the school roof!" cried Groovy Gran, hugging the delighted twins.

"And enough tattie scone scrumptiousness to feed all our fans," added Rab (including any fans who sneaked back for seconds and thirds and fourths and other fractions).

The hungry fans waved their arms and spoons in the air.

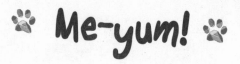 Me-yum!

"What a braw gig," said Scruff, waving the fans goodbye.

"Aye," said Biff, knitting a souvenir t-shirt.

"When will your next gig be?" Isla asked Rab.

He thought for a moment and glanced at his band mates.

"In thirty years!" they cried as one.

That's about 210 cat years, I meowed, working out the answer with my paws and claws. You can count on me to count on me.

27
Knock Knock!

One sunny Saturday a few weeks later, when Mum and Dad were back from their holiday and the kids were back at school, I explored the new roof. It wasn't creaky or leaky any more, thanks to all the cash raised by the Big Gig.

Suddenly I heard a

GRRRRR!

Was it another Dug o Doom out to get me? No, just my grumpy tummy rumbling. By the time you got to the end of this sentence I'd run back home.

"Here you are, Porridge," said Ross, tipping some delicious fishy biscuits into my mouth. "Eat up. You've got a lot to get through. Someone keeps sending you fishy biscuits in the post."

There was a KNOCK KNOCK at the front door.

"Who's there?" said Ross.

"Anita."

"Anita who?"

"Anita give you this package," said the postie. She handed over a bulky box and cycled off.

"That looks exciting," said Groovy Gran, riding up on a funky hover-trolley that Gadget Grandad had just invented.

"Let's see what's in the box," said Mum.

I slit through the cardboard with my claws and the sound of tasty tunes by the Tattie Scones filled the room.

 Me-wow!

"I've finally got a golden musical coat hanger!" cried Isla

"Me too!" yelled Ross.

"Me three!" chuckled Groovy Gran. "There's more than enough for everyone."

Except me.

"Nae, worries, Porridge. This is for you," said Ross. He handed me a golden cat bowl with my name inscribed on the side. "I guess you don't need a coat hanger as you never take off your coat."

Not even indoors, I purred.

I jumped in the empty cardboard box and made myself comfortable.

Who needs presents when you've got cardboard boxes? (It's a cat thing.)

"Porridge! There's a note stuck to your bahookie," giggled Isla.

Charming. I coolly flicked my tartan tail and the note spun into her hands. She read it out.

To the best pals a dug could ever hope to have. Thanks for a great night,

love Rab.

P.S. If you need any more coat hangers just ask.

P.P.S. Or fishy biscuits.

I really don't love being stuck in this box!

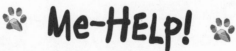

Me-HELP!

But I do love fishy biscuits.

Me-yum!

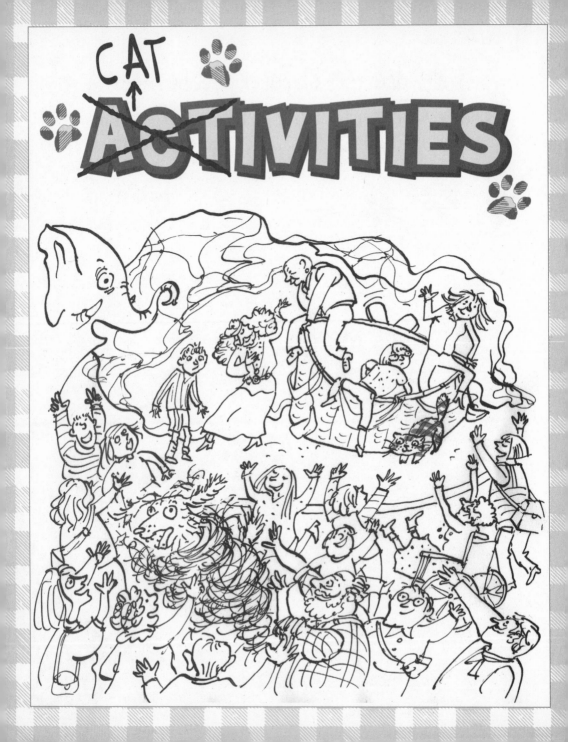

There are ten differences between these two pictures of **THE BIG GIG**. Can you spot them all?

And here are some of my favourite jokes...

What happened to the cat that swallowed a ball of wool?

It had mittens!

How many cats can you put into an empty Fishy Biscuit box?

Just one. After that, the box isn't empty!

What do cats wear at night?

Paw-jamas!

What fruit do the McFun twins like to eat?

Pears!